Dr. Prufrock's Wild Ride

Word problem: A brilliant and beautiful girl has only enough patience for three hours of irritation. Her annoying twin brother tells fibs about her for fifteen minutes the first night, twenty minutes the second night, twenty-five minutes the third night, and so on. How long will it take her to blow her top?

Never mind, I already know the answer.

My pain-in-the neck brother, Zeke, has already told you of our first adventures with the Undies (the people, not the unmentionables).

But before I report on what happened next, I've got to set the record straight. Typical Zeke, he's gotten it all wrong.

Also by Bruce Hale

THE UNDERWHERE SERIES
Prince of Underwhere
Flyboy of Underwhere

PiRATeS of UNDeRWHeRe

by BRUCE HALE

illustrated by
SHANE HILLMAN

HarperTrophy®
An Imprint of HarperCollins Publishers

Pirates of Underwhere
Text copyright © 2008 by Bruce Hale
Illustrations copyright © 2008 by Shane Hillman

Library of Congress Cataloging-in-Publication Data
Hale, Bruce.
Pirates of Underwhere / by Bruce Hale ; illustrated by Shane Hillman. — 1st ed.
p. cm.
Summary: Twins Stephanie and Zeke, their friend Hector, and cats Fitz and
Meathead once again venture into the world of Underwhere, this time look-
ing for the missing Brush of Wisdom, a magical item that looks suspiciously
like a jewelled toilet brush.
ISBN 978-0-06-085129-3
[1. Adventure and adventurers—Fiction. 2. Heroes—Fiction. 3. Magic—Fiction. 4. Cats—
Fiction. 5. Brothers and sisters—Fiction. 6. Twins—Fiction. 7. Humorous stories] I. Hillman,
Shane, ill. II. Title.
PZ7.H1295Pi 2008   2007014473
[Fic]—dc22   CIP
                                                        AC

Typography by Jennifer Heuer
❖
First Harper Trophy edition, 2009

To Sistah Marie,
with mucho aloha

PirATeS of UNDerWHERe

Dr. Prufrock's Wild Ride

Word problem: A brilliant and beautiful girl has only enough patience for three hours of irritation. Her annoying twin brother tells fibs about her for fifteen minutes the first night, twenty minutes the second night, twenty-five minutes the third night, and so on. How long will it take her to blow her top?

Never mind, I already know the answer.

My pain-in-the neck brother, Zeke, has already told you of our first adventures with the Undies (the people, not the unmentionables).

But before I report on what happened next,

1

I've got to set the record straight. Typical Zeke, he's gotten it all wrong.

Not the part about the zombies and the mini-dinosaurs, or our vow to help recover some magical objects and free the people of Underwhere from the UnderLord. That's correct.

But he makes me sound like some kind of priss who cares more about hair conditioner than about saving the world.

And *that's* just not true.

Using the proper conditioner *is* an important part of hair care. But it's not as important as keeping some evil dwarf from taking over your planet, okay?

And I'm so *not* a priss. Zeke and our neighbor Hector are typical boys; they never stop to think. I'm the sensible one. The one who says, "Gee, maybe we shouldn't jump into that shark-infested water with hands full of raw steak."

Can I help it if I always know the right thing to do?

Honestly.

But back to what happened next.

We were just getting home from school—Zeke and I and our neighbor Hector—when a wild-haired old man ran up our driveway. He looked like some kind of scientist. The mad kind.

"I need your help!" he cried. "My artifact is missing, and I'm afraid the UnderLord might have taken it."

"Let's go!" shouted Zeke.

"Wait," I said. "Who are *you*?"

The old man smoothed his hair. "Oh, I'm Dr. J. Robert Prufrock, a friend of your great-aunt Zenobia."

"Good enough for me," said Zeke.

I grabbed his arm. "But how do we know he's *really* a friend of Great-aunt Zenobia?"

Zeke rolled his eyes. "Duh, because he *said* so."

"That's right," said Hector. "And if Dr. Prufrock doesn't know whose friend he is, who would?" Good old Hector. He's cute, but he's as bad as Zeke.

"Remember 'stranger danger'?" I said. "Hello? Have you guys even heard a word of those lectures we've had since kindergarten?"

Dr. Prufrock held up his hands. "Children, please. Every minute counts."

I crossed my arms. "We don't know you, and besides, we really should do our homework first."

"Steph!" cried Hector and Zeke together.

"Well, we *should*," I said.

It always happens—I'm right, but they gang up on me.

Hector's orange cat, Fitz, wound around my ankles and grumbled. "Mrrow reer row *ree* roww."

"You too, kitty cat?" I said.

The white-haired man fumbled in his coat pockets. "By Odin's elbows," he muttered, "we're running out of . . . ah!"

"Running out of *ah*?" said Zeke.

Dr. Prufrock held out a photo. "*Now* do you believe me?"

The picture showed a cave mouth and three really old people in khaki pants: Dr. Prufrock, some lady with a pinched face, and our great-aunt Zenobia.

"Looks like Indiana Jones's grandparents," said Hector.

"I resent that," said Dr. Prufrock. "Who's Indiana Jones?"

Zeke tapped the photo. "See, I told you. They're friends."

"Okay," I said. "But this better be quick."

Dr. Prufrock hustled us into his car, a dented gray thing. I brushed off the front seat carefully before getting in. Fitz hopped onto my lap.

With a roar, the car belched smoke and poked down the street.

This was not going to be quick.

Dr. Prufrock filled us in. "I need help, and I can't trust anyone outside our little circle."

He took the corner too sharply, and I was smushed into the side door.

"Of the three people in that photograph," he continued, "Zenobia is gone, and Amelia is in hiding. If I can't trust Zenny's family, whom can I trust?"

Zenny? I thought. Had they been boyfriend and girlfriend, finding love among the ruins?

Awww . . . how romantic. Even wrinkled love is kind of sweet.

"How can we help, Dr. Prufrock?" I asked.

"What do you know about the UnderLord?" said the old man.

He pulled into the oncoming lane to pass a school bus. Drivers honked and slammed on their brakes. Fitz's claws dug into my leg.

Zeke clung to the seat back. "He was trying to take over our world."

"By posing as the rapper Beefy D," Hector added.

"Suffering Socrates! It's worse than I thought," said the doctor.

Hector smirked. "And you didn't even hear him rap."

Distracted, Dr. Prufrock drove over the curb and sideswiped a trash can. Don't they ever make old people take driving tests? Honestly.

Then something struck me. "Wait, have you been to Underwhere?"

"With Amelia and Zenobia," he said. "That's where we found the artifacts."

"What artifacts?" said Zeke.

"The Throne, the Brush, and the Scepter," said the doctor. "And by all that's holy, they must not fall back into the UnderLord's hands."

He stomped on the brakes, and the car sputtered to a halt.

"Ah, home, sweet home."

Dr. Prufrock's house was a lot like him—tall, messy, and needing a new coat of paint. What is it about guys and dirt?

He led us through the front door and down a dusty hall. "I last saw it here, in the library."

We peeked into a room. Books lined the walls and rose from the floor in piles like ruined towers. A sea of papers lapped around them. Crusty dishes and coffee mugs sat everywhere—some with flies, some without. Rumpled clothes, empty shoe boxes, three chessboards, a stuffed anaconda, and a full suit of rusty armor completed the picture.

"Um, Dr. Prufrock?" I said.

"Yes, Stephanie?"

"Are you sure you haven't just *misplaced* your artifact?"

He frowned and looked about. "Er . . . well, yes, pretty sure."

Zeke put his hands on his hips. "So . . . what are we looking for?"

"Well," said Dr. Prufrock, "the artifact looks rather like a common toilet brush."

Hector and Zeke snickered. I could have predicted that.

"Only it's larger and painted with colorful runes," said the doctor.

Hector gazed out the window. "Has it also got golden bristles?" he asked.

"Yes," said Dr. Prufrock.

"And is it about *so* long?" Hector held his hands apart.

"Why, yes."

"With some kind of sparkly ring around the handle?"

"That's it exactly!" said the doctor. "Do you see it?"

Hector pointed outside. "Sure, it's in that cat's mouth."

Cat Burglar

We ran to the glass and peered into the backyard. Hector was right. In the shaggy grass sat a familiar, fat brown cat with a fancy toilet brush in his mouth.

"Isn't that *your* cat?" said Hector.

"Meathead?" said Zeke.

"Meathead!" I cried.

"Mrrow!" said Fitz.

Meathead looked up at us.

He had run off a few weeks ago. I always expected Meathead to return sometime. But never with his own toilet brush. (He wasn't exactly a clean kitty.)

Zeke pounded toward the half-open back door, Hector and I right on his heels. We burst out onto a porch.

"Slow down!" I hissed. "You'll spook him."

For once—a miracle—Zeke listened. He stopped short. "H-e-e-e-re, Meathead," he said. "N-i-i-i-i-ce kitty. Give us the brushy-wushy."

Meathead backed up a step.

I elbowed Zeke aside. "Let *me* do it. He probably remembers the time you painted stripes on him."

"What do you mean?" said Zeke. "Meathead *liked* playing skunk."

I sat on the steps and held out a friendly hand. "Here, kitty kitty."

Meathead blinked. But he didn't drop the brush.

Slowly and carefully, I got to my feet.

"Easy now," said Dr. Prufrock from behind us.

We crept forward.

The cat backed up another step.

"Good thing ol' Meatbrain doesn't know how valuable that thing is," Zeke said.

Meathead's ears pricked up. Brush in mouth, he turned and trotted for the side yard.

"Brilliant move, basket case!" I cried, giving chase.

"What'd I do?" said Zeke, joining me.

I spared him a glance. "Fitz can understand English; why do you think Meathead can't?"

Meathead plunged into the overgrown bushes beside the house, the tip of his tail wriggling through the jungle—probably all poison ivy and prickly plants. (Dr. Prufrock's gardening was about equal to his housekeeping.) We waded through the bushes anyway.

"Give us the brush, fleaball!" cried Zeke.

"That's it, genius," I said. "Sweet-talk him."

Meathead reappeared on the far side of the thicket and bolted across the front lawn. Ten seconds later we followed, running full out.

And we might have caught him too—if not for the two hairy, black-suited men blocking our path.

"Greetings, children," said the chubbier man.

"Can't talk now," said Zeke, dodging past. The taller man snagged his arm.

"Hold on," said the man. A monster-sized mole on his cheek made it hard to look him in the eyes. (Or into the sunglasses that covered his eyes.)

It was our old friends, the nameless spies from H.U.S.H., an agency so secret, even *they* didn't know what H.U.S.H. stood for. They had forced us to spy in Underwhere. We called them Agent Belly and Agent Mole.

And they were anything but friends.

"Let's talk," said Agent Belly.

From the sidewalk just beyond them, Meathead turned to watch.

"Sorry, but we have to catch our cat," I said.

"No," growled Agent Mole, "you don't."

Hector flinched. I glanced back at the house for help, only to see Dr. Prufrock duck behind a curtain. Where's a grown-up when you need one?

"Um, maybe we can spare a minute," I said.

Meathead ambled away with the brush, tail held jauntily, mocking us.

"Aww, *sheesh*," said Zeke.

Agent Belly adjusted his fake black beard. Mole straightened a fake mustache. I suppose they thought their disguises were good. And maybe they were—for a kindergartner.

"Children," said Belly, "we appreciated the, er, magic rock you brought back from your last trip below."

Magic rock. A nice description for the dhownaught, an enchanted stone that would happily bite your hand off.

"It had our team quite fascinated," he continued. "But now . . ."

"Need more," grunted Agent Mole.

Belly smiled. "Yes, the rock isn't enough. We want something better."

"Like what?" asked Zeke. He looked where Meathead had gone. Mole tightened his grip.

"An object of power," said Agent Belly. "You know, a wand, a crystal, a gizmo that people down there use for making magic?"

Zeke, Hector, and I traded glances. We knew that Meathead was carrying a power object. But we didn't want to just hand it over to the men from H.U.S.H. when our friends in Underwhere needed it so badly.

I chewed my lip. Soon Meathead would be long gone.

"That brush," I said.

"No!" said Zeke.

"Speak," said Agent Mole.

"That brush our cat was carrying? It's a power object."

Agent Belly smirked. "A *toilet* brush? You must think your government likes to hire fools."

"It's true," said Hector. Mole glared. Hector held up a hand. "I mean, not true that we think you're fools—true that the brush is magic."

Agent Belly scratched under his fake beard. "Come now, children."

Typical grown-ups. They didn't believe us when we told the truth. Fine. I knew how to deal with that attitude.

"That's right, Hector," I said, meaningfully. "A land with enchanted rocks couldn't *possibly* produce a magic toilet brush. Stop pretending."

Hector frowned. Then he got it. "Ri-i-ight. *That* brush isn't magic."

"It isn't?" said Zeke, clueless as usual.

I elbowed him. "Of *course* it isn't."

"Not so fast," said Agent Belly. "You can't slip one over on us."

Mole nodded. "Go get the brush."

"And don't disappoint us," said the chubby spy. "It would be a shame if you flunked out of elementary school because your grades suddenly plunged."

"Our *grades*?" I said, gripping my skirt. "But you can't change our grades."

"Can't we?" said Belly. "The government computer network is a marvelous thing." He smiled and gave us a finger wave. "Ta, ta."

Mole released Zeke. We took off running.

In a flash, we hit the sidewalk and sprinted to the corner. The streets ran in four directions.

All four were cat free.

"Dang!" said Zeke. "Now we'll *never* find him."

"Not necessarily," said Hector.

I turned to him. "What do you mean?"

"Oh, *Fitzie!*" he called.

His cat popped out of the hedge and padded up to us. "Mrrrow reow?"

"How'd you like to earn a bowl of Tuna Cat Chow?" asked Hector.

Fitz looked unimpressed. He was good at it.

"*Fresh* tuna?" said Hector.

Fitz rolled his eyes.

"Okay," said Hector. "You win. A whole side of salmon."

Fitz purred. "Murr reer roor?" he asked.

Hector waved a hand at the empty intersection. "Follow that cat!"

Sniffing the breeze, Fitz took the left-hand street. We followed.

Two houses down, he froze and stared at some bushes. His tail twitched.

"Is it Meathead?" I asked.

Fitz sank into a crouch. The bushes rustled. Something parted the grass.

A field mouse.

"Fitz!" Hector pulled on the cat's collar. "I said *cat*, not *mouse*."

Fitz gave him a baleful look, but he got back on track.

Three houses down, he squeezed through a half-open gate into a construction site.

A rotten-egg smell greeted us, stronger than the funk from Zeke's dirty laundry pile. Something about it seemed familiar.

"Hey, isn't this where we came out after our first trip to Underwhere?" I said.

Zeke looked around. "I never thought I'd say these words, but you're right."

The structure was more complete than when we'd last been here, a week earlier. It was as odd as the building going up near our house—all lopsided and oversized. But here the walls were solid, and windows glinted from the top story.

Fitz stepped through the cavelike entrance. He made for a corner room.

"That's the tunnel we came up through," said Hector.

We stopped in the doorway. A strong wind plucked at our clothes. It blew from a dark hole in the center of the floor.

Fitz sat and looked up at us, then at the hole.

"Down there?" I said.

"*That's* where Meathead went?" said Zeke.

The cat gave him a *well, duh* stare—the same kind I often give my brother.

Zeke and I looked at each other. *Oh, boy.*

"Okay," he said. "Down the hatch."

21

As he walked over and slid down the portal, I thought, *I picked a fine day to wear a skirt.*

Then I clapped my hands to my thighs, and down I went after him.

CHAPTER 3

OKAY, FITZ. LEAD US TO MEATHEAD!

DO I *LOOK* LIKE A GREAT SLOBBERY DOG?

UH, NO.

THEN STOP *TREATING* ME LIKE ONE. I DON'T *TRACK*, I DON'T *PLAY DEAD*, AND YOU'D BETTER *BELIEVE* I DON'T *FETCH*.

COME ON, ZEKE. YOU CAN'T ARGUE WITH A CAT.

RUSTLE RUSTLE

MEATHEAD?

YAAAH! DINOSAURS!

THEY'LL EAT US ALIVE!

HOLD STILL!

APATOSAURUSES ARE **PLANT** EATERS. THEY WON'T HURT YOU.

WHUMP!

OW!

NOT *MUCH*, ANYWAY.

DOWN, BOY!

ON _THAT?_

WOT'S WRONG WITH THE _RAFT?_

NOTHING! IT'S JUST, UH... SHOULDN'T A PRINCE AND PRINCESS TRAVEL ON SOMETHING A BIT MORE... _DIGNIFIED?_

CASTIN' OFF!

SO WHY'S THIS PORT SUCH A _BIG DEAL?_

PORT 'EINIE CONTROLS THIS _RIVER._ AND THE RIVER CONTROLS OUR _SUPPLIES._

NO PORT 'EINIE, _NO FOOD!_

LUCKILY, IT *DOESN'T SEE* TOO WELL.

HISSSSH!!

IS SHE FRIENDLY?

SHE'S A *HE*, LUV. THE *SHE-*SERPENT'S ON THE OTHER—

WHO CARES? IT'S A STUPID, UGLY *SEA SERPENT.*

SHH!

WHAT'S WRONG?

'E MAY NOT *SEE* TOO WELL, BUT 'E 'EARS JUST FINE.

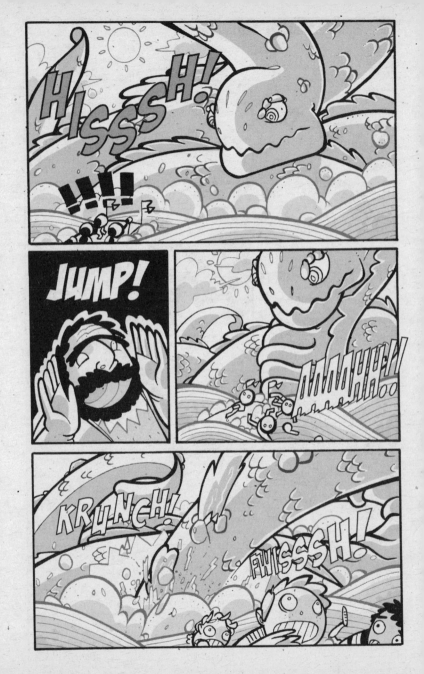

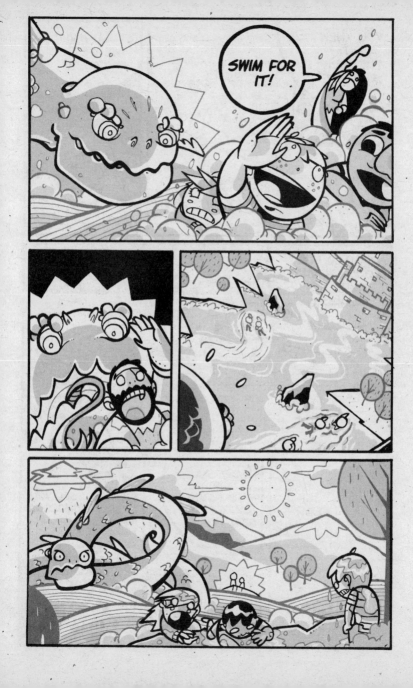

YOU KNEW ABOUT THE *SEA SERPENT?*

OH, AYE!

THEN *WHY* DID WE GET SO *CLOSE?*

WANTED YOU TO KNOW WHAT WE'RE UP AGAINST.

YOU COULDN'T HAVE DRAWN US A *PICTURE?*

WE AWAIT YOUR *PLAN!*

HERE'S A PLAN: FIND SOME *BOATS*— SOME *REAL* BOATS!

SEE YOU TOMORROW!

GREAT. *NOW* WE HAVE TO *WALK* ALL THE WAY BACK. SOAKING WET.

SQUISH SQUOSH

A FLYING HORSE!

CHAPTER
4

Mighty Mouth

Probability problem: If a live-in babysitter is in a bad mood 70 percent of the time, a blah mood 20 percent, a good mood 10 percent, and a talkative mood *all* the time, what is the chance that two kids who miss dinner will get royally chewed out?

If they live in *our* house, 100 percent.

As I predicted, we got home late. And as I predicted, cousin Caitlyn, who babysits while our parents are off on digs, was upset.

Sometimes I get tired of being right.

"I'm gonna so totally *kill* you little blivets!"

Caitlyn yelled as we stepped through the door. "In fact, after I kill you, I'm gonna, like, bring you back to life as zombies, so I can have the pleasure of killing you again! Where *were* you smigmotes, anyway? Having your brains drained?"

Caitlyn usually has a lot to say.

"We —," I began.

"It's six o'clock," she interrupted. "*Six!* And what time did I say to be home by?" She pointed her cell phone at us like a sword.

"Um, five?" said Zeke.

Then our cousin noticed our appearance for the first time. "And what's with the monzo-scrunge look? Did you, like, crawl home through the sewers?"

"Actually," I said, "we—"

"I made dinner for you little zimwats, and now it's cold." Caitlyn paced up and down the living

46

room. "I'm not Suzie Q. Homemaker here. I'm not Betty Crocker. I'm your cousin. And your parents aren't paying me enough to cook your dinner *and* warm it up for you! That's, like, double duty!"

"We're really, *really* sorry," I said.

"Sorry doesn't cut the mayonnaise," said Caitlyn, crossing her arms. "You two are *so* grounded."

"*Grounded!?*" cried Zeke.

"For the whole weekend. I'm going to miss a totally weehawken party, but it'll be worth it to see your miserable faceplates going boo-hoo-hoo."

"But you can't *do* that," said Zeke. He never knows when to shut up.

Caitlyn grinned, a bad sign. "Oh, really?" she said. "*I'm* in charge here, dinky doodle, and I think I've been way too easy on you. I'm giving Steffo the night off, and you're on dish patrol."

"Sheesh," said Zeke.

"Now get in there and eat your cold meat loaf," she said. "March!"

I could have told him. It's no good arguing with Caitlyn when she's in that mood. Or any mood, really. We marched.

After dinner, I studied my math book while Zeke cleaned the dishes (although the way *he* does them, I wouldn't have been surprised if they ended up dirtier than when he started). Reviewing modes, means, and averages would be a big help if I got picked for the Mathletes team on Monday.

(Not to be cocky, but I knew Mrs. Ricotta would pick me. I *am* her best math student, after all.)

With homework double-checked, I switched the TV onto the news.

"Whatcha watching?" came Zeke's voice from

behind. "Something boring?"

"The news, Midget Boy," I said. "Some of us like to know what's going on."

"Hah!" He flopped down on the couch. "What's going on is you're kissing up to Caitlyn. And I—"

"I'm not *listening*," I said, turning up the volume.

". . . newest benefactor," the blond reporter was saying. "Today he promised our town a new skating rink and amusement park. And why?"

The camera showed a close-up of a moonfaced man wearing a huge cowboy hat. "It's cuz ah purely lur-r-v-v-ve this town," he drawled. "All of y'all are sweeter than a heap of pecan pie ice-cream sundaes with—"

Zeke snatched the remote. "*Bo*-ring." He clicked to the cartoon channel.

"Give it over, dwarf!" I said.

"Never, dweeb!"

I reached for the remote control. He held me off with one hand and kept the remote behind him.

"Wart!"

"Dorkus maximus!"

Caitlyn's voice cut through the shouting. "Shut it, blivets! I'm trying to do my political science project, and all I hear is your 'mamma gamma blamma.' You just volunteered for deep cleaning the whole house—*both* of you."

"But he—," I began.

Our cousin loomed in the doorway, hands on hips. "You can start tomorrow by vacuuming and shampooing the carpet."

I glared at Zeke.

He turned so Caitlyn couldn't see and stuck his tongue out at me.

Honestly.

I blew out a sigh. It was going to be a long weekend.

By Sunday night, my whole body reeked of ammonia and lemon, even my hair. Yuck. My fingers were red and raw, like grated hot dogs.

Zeke and I were finishing up the living room. We had hardly spoken all weekend—a big relief.

While he dusted a bowl of glass fruit, I tidied up the books and magazines. And that's when I found *The Book of Booty*, the collection of mystical predictions we had brought back from Underwhere.

I flipped through it. The faint stink of rotten eggs rose from its pages.

"No fair reading when I'm doing all the work," said Zeke. He tossed a glass apple in the air.

"Careful!" I said. I swear Zeke was absent the day they handed out brains.

"Yeah, yeah."

I held up the book. "I was just wondering about Dr. Prufrock's brush, what it can . . . hey, here it is." I noticed the drawing of a fancy toilet brush with golden bristles.

Zeke joined me. "What's it say?"

I read, "'. . . And yea, though the Booty be fruity, the Lost Prince shall shake it.'"

Zeke frowned. "What's a fruity booty?"

"Never mind," I said. "I'll skip ahead . . . ah, here we go: 'The Brush of Wisdom shows the truth/ though it be hidden, rough, or smooth.'"

"*Truth* and *smooth* don't rhyme," said Zeke.

"Yeah, but *Zeke* and *freak* do," I said. "'If you would know a thing completely/ brush it thrice and brush it sweetly. Lies cannot withstand the push/ not when it comes from Wisdom's Brush.'"

"And *push* and *brush* don't rhyme either," said Zeke, flipping the page. "Whoever wrote this is a worse rapper than Beefy D."

I put the book down. "Don't you get it? This brush is powerful magic. With it, you can learn the true nature of anything."

"Huh," said Zeke.

"And you know where this magical brush is right now?"

"In Meathead's mouth," said Zeke.

"Somehow," I said, "that doesn't seem like a good thing."

CHAPTER 5

The Guy with the Golden Touch

I don't know why Zeke attracts bullies. Maybe it's because he's shorter than average. Or maybe it's because of that look in his eyes.

(Oh, wait—I know. It's because he's thoroughly and completely obnoxious.)

Whatever the reason, they found him at recess.

I was chatting with my friend Heather on the swings. Zeke and Hector were tossing a football nearby. Or to be more accurate, they were chasing it. My brother's not exactly a football hero.

Then trouble showed up.

Trouble in the shape of Melvin Prang and his sidekick Darryl.

"Hey, Darryl," said Melvin, acting all puzzled. "I didn't know they had a new football league at school."

"What league is that?" said Darryl.

"The inky-dinky league!" Melvin shoved Zeke and snatched the football.

Zeke's face fell. "Come on, Melvin," he said. "Give it back."

The bully tossed it to Darryl. "*I* don't have it."

Zeke slouched over to the sidekick. "Darryl . . ."

Darryl threw it back to Melvin. "*I* don't have it."

These mental giants probably would've kept up their game all through recess, if not for the custodian.

"Hey, Prang!" called Mr. Wheener. "And uh, you." He pointed at Darryl. "Come here."

Darryl dropped the ball like it had burned his fingers.

"We wasn't doing nothing," said Melvin. (Honestly. So few bullies speak proper English.)

Zeke grinned.

Melvin stabbed a thick finger at him. "Not one word, shrimp!"

As they approached the janitor, Hector said, "Wow, Wheener to the rescue!"

"It's pronounced *Veener*," I said.

"*Vhatever*." Hector snickered.

"I'm sorry I ever made fun of him," said Zeke. "Mr. Wheener's actually punishing them."

The custodian talked to the bullies. We were too far away to overhear. But after they spoke for a minute, all three looked over at Zeke. Then Mr. Wheener smiled and patted Melvin's shoulder.

The janitor and bullies shook hands. Then they went their separate ways.

"Doesn't look like punishment to me," Hector said.

. . .

After recess, the school held a surprise assembly. Everyone gathered on the grass before a portable stage. Because our class arrived late, we ended up way over on the side, where a tall speaker system blocked my view.

". . . to thank our new friend," the principal, Ms. Johnson, was saying. "From the goodness of his heart, he's buying us a new computer lab full of top-notch equipment."

I perked up. New computers? This would put me one step closer to my goal of being the world's first female computer genius and all-around billionaire.

"He'll be telling your parents about his big plans at this week's town meeting," said Ms. Johnson, "but right now, please give him a warm welcome. Boys and girls, let's hear it for Bobby Bob Moxenboxer!"

Why do grown-ups always expect us to cheer for someone we don't know?

My classmates gave the kind of polite applause you'd expect. A man in a huge cowboy hat took the mike. He was short and wore an electric blue suit.

"Mah dear friends," said Mr. Moxenboxer. "Bobby Bob feels pleased as punch to be able to help you darlin' little ankle biters."

Zeke leaned across Heather. "Hey, isn't this the guy from the TV?"

"I can't tell," I said, craning for a better look. "But he sounds the same."

"Bobby Bob's as tickled as an armadillo in saw grass," the cowboy said. "These danged computers will help create the workers of tomorrow today."

He said a few other things. Possibly boring things. My classmates gossiped, and I confess I started day-dreaming about making the Mathletes team.

But then Mr. Moxenboxer said something

that grabbed everybody's attention.

". . . So ol' Bobby Bob has got a li'l ol' *giftie* for you."

The blue-suited cowboy reached into a sack and flung a fistful of gold coins at us. Kids screamed and fought to catch the money.

Someone even pulled my hair—the nerve! (I suspected Melvin.)

Ms. Johnson stepped forward. "Um, I'm not sure this is appropriate—"

Bobby Bob scooped up another handful of gold and flung it at the teachers sitting in folding chairs. They almost trampled each other going after the coins.

The principal's protest died out. I smoothed my hair.

Then I got a good look at our visitor, and my mouth fell open. He was short, he was moonfaced . . .

"Um, Zeke, who does Bobby Bob remind you of?"

"I dunno, Santa Claus?" he said.

"Look closer, genius," I said. "How many grown-ups are shorter than you?"

He looked. And then he gaped.

"The UnderLord!" we said together.

Grabbing the money bag in both hands, the phony Mr. Moxenboxer emptied it into the crowd of kids. He yelled, "Let's hear it for Bobby Bob. Hip, hip . . ."

The audience went wild. "*Hoooo*-rawww!"

"Class dismissed!" shouted Mr. Moxenboxer.

The mess that followed reminded me of the time Zeke lit a firecracker in an anthill. Kids and teachers swarmed the field, battling over stray coins.

But Zeke and I stayed planted. Two thoughts ran through my mind: What was the UnderLord up to? And how could we stop him?

The moment I'd been waiting for came just before lunch. Our teacher, Mrs. Ricotta, cleared her throat.

"And now," she said, "I'm sure you're all eager to hear which members of this class will be joining the Mathletes."

"Math *dweebs*, you mean," said Melvin Prang.

"That's enough, Melvin," said Mrs. Ricotta. She looked around the room. "Our class will contribute three team members this year: Amir, Heather, and . . ." She looked right at me. "Stephanie."

My face went hot, and I might have squealed.

"Congratulations to you all," said Mrs. Ricotta.

My classmates clapped. I didn't even care that most of them didn't mean it.

Me, a Mathlete!

Then Mrs. Ricotta brought me back down to

earth with a thump. "We'll be practicing after school all week," she said, "in preparation for Friday's meet."

Zeke shot me a look.

Uh-oh.

How could I be in Mathletes and help the Undies, both?

Mrs. R dismissed us for lunch. I stepped outside to drink from the water fountain and think.

Heather came up and hugged me. "I'm so glad we're both Mathletes," she said. "We rock!"

"Yay, us," I said limply.

She ran off to tell her other friends.

Zeke shuffled up, tight lipped. "So," he said. "You're gonna blow off this whole Mathletes thing, right?"

I shrugged. "It's kind of a big deal."

"But you can't do it," said Zeke. "We promised the Undies."

My back stiffened. "*You* promised the Undies."

Hector arrived and noticed our expressions. "Okay, what's up?"

"She's leaving us for the Math geeks," said Zeke.

My fists clenched. "I didn't *say* that."

Zeke leaned toward me. "Why bother with that dumb team anyway? Math is totally worthless."

"Oh, *really*?" I said. "I bet you I can *prove* how useful it is."

"You're on," said Zeke. "Let's go, Hector. We're too dumb to hang out with Little Miss Einstein."

"Fine," I said. "Go."

But it wasn't fine. As I watched them leave, my stomach felt all knotted up.

This was a tough puzzle, like some kind of wicked-tricky Venn diagram. Helping the Undies was in one circle; being in Mathletes was in another. *Hmm.* Was there a place where the two circles intersected, where I could do both?

"Hey, new Mathlete!" called Mrs. Ricotta from the doorway. "Working on a problem?"

"As a matter of fact, I am." I turned to her. "Mrs. R, do you think I could have a little time off next period?"

"Of course, Stephanie. What for?"

"Oh," I said, smiling, "it's a . . . special project."

CHAPTER 6

PRRRRRR

OH, ALL *RIGHT.* DEAL.

HE WENT THIS-A-WAY, BUT IT SMELLS LIKE YOUR VILE CAT IS LONG GONE.

DOESN'T MATTER. *MEAT-HEAD* *ALWAYS* DOES THE SAME THING.

SHREDS YOUR LIVING ROOM DRAPES? LEAVES *GIFTS* IN YOUR SHOES?

BESIDES THAT. HE ALWAYS...

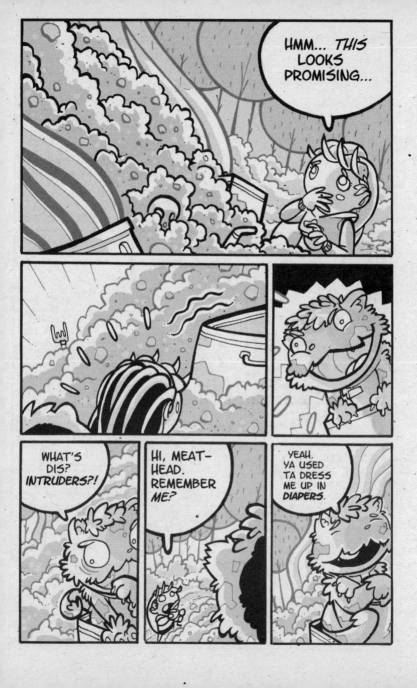

MY *CAT* IS WORKING FOR THE UNDERLORD?

HE ALWAYS DID HAVE A *SHIFTY* LOOK.

RUMBLE DUMBLE

WHAT'S *THAT?*

ALF! *HEY,* ALF!

PRINCESS? WOT ARE *YOU* DOING AT THE *DUMP?*

GETTING THE *BRUSH OF WISDOM.*

WELL DONE, YOUR 'IGHNESS.

HUH. FUNNY WHAT SOME FOLKS THROW AWAY.

LISTEN, COULD YOU TAKE ME TO *PORT HEINIE?* I'M IN A BIT OF A HURRY.

ONE WAGON RIDE LATER...

'ERE'S THE DAM.

SEE?

CAN'T APPROACH BY *LAND.* GOTTA COME BY *WATER.*

WITH A *SEA MONSTER* ON EITHER SIDE.

OH, AYE.

HOW DOES THE UNDERLORD *KEEP* THEM THERE?

THE *UNDERLORD?!* THE SNAKEYS DON'T WORK FOR THE LIKES OF 'IM.

THEN *WHY* DO THEY STAY?

OF A SORT. 'E'S *BLOODY FRED*, THE PIRATE.

A PIRATE?

OH, AYE.

WE'LL MEET HIM TOMORROW. I'VE GOT TO GET BACK. MATHLETES IS CALLING.

WOT, THEM LITTLE NUMBERS CAN *TALK* TO YOU?

UM, SOMETHING LIKE THAT.

TCH, I'LL NEVER UNDERSTAND ROYALTY.

CHAPTER 7

Backyard Zombie

Logic problem: In the struggle for control of the world, there are a) good guys; b) bad guys; and c) quite a few guys who seem bad but might be good or seem good but might be bad, depending. Which ones can you trust?

That was the question of the day. Zeke, Hector, and I were sitting in our living room trying to answer it.

"I still say we should call Dr. Prufrock," said Zeke. "He *was* our great-aunt's friend."

"We *think*," I said. "But I don't know. There's something fishy about him."

He leaned forward. "Would you rather call the spies?"

"H.U.S.H.?" I said.

"Don't shush me," said Zeke.

"I meant the spies."

"Oh," said Zeke.

Hector stood. "Look, we should do this on our own. We've got the Throne, and now the Brush, thanks to Steph . . ."

I shrugged modestly. "You're welcome."

"So let's just figure out how they work, figure out this Bobby Bob UnderLord's game, and stop him at the town meeting."

"One problem," said Zeke.

"Yes?" I asked.

"How are we going to *get to* that meeting way across town?"

"Ah," said Hector. "Hadn't thought of that." We all fell silent.

And in the silence, I heard a voice in the next room: "Shut *up*. That is totally bazongoid. No *way* she's, like, giving us another poli-sci project!"

Caitlyn.

I smiled. "I know who has wheels."

"Caitlyn?" said Zeke. "She'd *never* take us there."

"She will if she thinks it'll get her a better grade in political science class."

Hector frowned. "But why would she believe that?"

"Leave it to me," I said.

Somehow I managed to convince Caitlyn not only to take us to the town meeting the day after next, but also to let us go work on a school project over at Hector's house right away. How? I'm the smarter twin.

On the way over to Hector's we kept a sharp

lookout for spies, UnderLords, and stray doctors. The place seemed deserted. Way down the twilit street, a familiar-looking kid rode a bike. Across the lawn, Fitz was stalking a bird.

Other than that, no one.

"Let's hit the backyard," said Hector.

We passed through the gate. I noticed that the Throne—this weird-looking Undie toilet our aunt Zenobia left us—was sitting by the plastic wading pool.

"You moved it?" I asked.

"Grandma said it didn't go with the drapes," said Hector.

Zeke unwrapped the Brush from the T-shirt I'd covered it with. "Now how do we test this?"

"*The Book of Booty* says if you rub something three times with the Brush, you learn its true nature," I said.

"Okay," said Zeke, waving it at me. "Who

wants a brushing?"

"I swear, Zeke, if you touch my hair with that thing . . . !"

Hector reached into his pocket and held up a coin. "How about this?"

"Is that gold?" said Zeke. "Ice cream's on *you.*" He stroked the Brush across the coin—once, twice, three times. Nothing happened.

"So," said Hector. "The true nature of a gold coin is a gold coin?"

Something rustled in the bushes.

"What's that?" I said.

"Probably just Fitz," said Hector. He glanced down at the coin. "Hey, check it out."

The gold was fading to a dull gray. And the engraving was changing too—from a president's profile to a pair of undies.

"'One boxer buck,'" Hector read, from the inscription. "'In shorts we trust.'"

"Dang," said Zeke. "There goes our ice cream."

A thought struck me. "Did you get that coin from that fake Bobby Bob?"

Hector nodded. "The UnderLord is passing out phony money? But why?"

"I don't know," I said. "But I bet we'll find out at that town meeting."

"And what do we do until then?" said Zeke. His eyes lit up. "Hey, let's test the Brush on something better." His gaze went to the Throne.

Holding the Brush at arm's length, Zeke rubbed the Throne's seat once, twice, three times. He stepped back.

I held my breath.

Slowly, ever so slowly, the rim of the seat began to glow blue. The light grew brighter and brighter.

Just then, Fitz burst from the bushes, hot on the heels of a lizard. It scuttled up the Throne and into the bowl. Fitz was right behind it.

"*No, Fitzie!*" cried Hector. He scooped up the cat in his arms.

"Mrr reeuw *rauw*," yowled Fitz.

"Uh-uh," said Zeke. "Bad for kitties."

The Throne's light grew so bright it hurt my eyes. Then—*foof!*— it winked out.

Two scaly feet emerged from the Throne. A head followed.

"Is that the same lizard?" asked Hector.

"No, it's the Potty Gecko!" Zeke snickered.

I rolled my eyes. "Real dignified, Prince of Underwhere."

"I'm serious," said Hector. "It looks different."

We all leaned forward. The lizard seemed bigger, darker. And its eyes had a strange dull gleam.

"*Hhraaagh!*" it hissed, biting at my nose.

"Yah!" I shrieked. We all jumped back.

But the lizard kept coming. Slowly, step by step, it followed us. That steady march reminded me of something.

"*Meeurr!*" Fitz wriggled free of Hector's arms and bolted for the kitty door.

The lizard turned to chase him, but at a turtle's pace.

And suddenly I knew: "It's a *zombie* lizard!" I said. "The Throne creates zombies."

"Whoaah!" came a cry from the bushes. Branches cracked as something heavy landed.

"Who's there?" cried Hector.

"Agent Belly?" said Zeke.

No reply. A body crashed through the bushes and thumped against the wooden fence.

"Come on out!" I said.

Whoever it was, he or she was climbing the fence.

Hector and Zeke looked at each other. "Come on," said Zeke.

They dashed to the gate, with me right behind

them. We hit the lawn just in time to see the boy on a bicycle disappear around the corner.

"And don't come back!" Hector shouted.

Zeke looked thoughtful.

"What is it?" I asked.

"Call me crazy," he said. "But that back looked a lot like Melvin's."

I twisted my hair into a ponytail. "You're crazy. And I hope you're wrong."

Zeke winced. "So do I, frizz head. So do I."

CHAPTER 8

The Brush-Off

After some effort, we managed to catch the zombie lizard in a bottle. Fitz kept staring at it with round yellow eyes.

Since someone had seen the Throne in action, we figured we'd better move it. Hector, Zeke, and I lugged the thing back to our house. We left it in the backyard under a blue tarp.

The Brush we stashed in my dad's office—a room so messy, small animals have disappeared in it.

At school the next day, Zeke and I kept eyeing Melvin and the other boys in class. Which one was the spy? And what would he do with his knowledge?

When second recess rolled around, I waited until the classroom emptied to talk to Mrs. Ricotta. I hate to have an audience for bad news.

"I, uh, need to miss part of Mathletes practice today," I said.

Her brown eyes looked concerned. "Is something wrong?"

"No, it's—well, *yes*," I said. "I mean, not *wrong*, exactly, but it *will* be, if—"

I hated to lie to Mrs. R. But how do you tell your teacher you need time off to save the Undies?

"Mathletes is a very serious commitment," she said.

"I know that." I twisted a pencil in my hands.

"I can't have my people dropping out for any old reason," said Mrs. Ricotta. "It wouldn't be fair to the team."

"*Please*," I said. "Just this once."

She bit her lip. "Well, all right. This one time. But

90

you finish your business quickly and come right here."

"Thanks, Mrs. R.!" I said. "You're the best!"

I rushed outside to tell Zeke and Hector. They were sitting on a low wall by the basketball courts, looking glum.

"Cheer up!" I said. "Mrs. Ricotta's going to let me miss part of practice today. I can come meet the pirates in Underwhere."

Zeke barely looked up. Hector said, "That's nice."

"Wait a minute," I said. "Where's the happy? What's going on?"

"He lost it," said Hector.

"Lost what?" I said. "His mind? His looks? Don't worry—he's never had 'em to lose."

Zeke sank his head in his hands. "The Brush," he muttered.

"You're kidding," I said. "Right?"

Hector shook his head.

"But the Brush is safe at home in Dad's office."

"*Was,*" said Zeke.

I clenched my jaw. "What did you do, dwarf brain?"

"I, uh, used it on my homework last night—just to check the answers."

"You *what?*" I cried. "That's cheating!"

He looked up. "I didn't *mean* to cheat. It was just an experiment. And it gave me all the right answers."

Hector smirked. "That's a first."

"So?" I said. "Then you brought it to school. What for?"

Zeke's shoulders slumped. "A lie detector."

"Huh?" I crinkled my forehead.

"He rubbed it on Melvin," said Hector.

"You *didn't!*" I said.

"I did."

"Then he asked Melvin if he'd been spying on us," Hector continued.

"You didn't!" I said.

"I did."

"Then Melvin grabbed the Brush, hit Zeke, and stole it," Hector finished.

"He didn't!" I said, pushing Zeke with both hands.

"Ow!" he cried. "Stop shoving! *He* stole it, not me."

I fumed. Of all the hare-brained, numbskulled bozos, my brother had to be the harey-brainiest and numbskulliest.

"But Melvin would never have swiped it if you hadn't taken it from home and brushed him with it!" I said.

"She's got a point," said Hector.

Zeke rose and paced. "What'll we do?"

"Go ask him to give it back," I said.

"Are you *nuts*?" said Zeke. "He won't even give me back a football."

"But if you ask nicely, he might give you a black eye," said Hector.

I crossed my arms. "Why don't we *all* go ask him for it—together?"

They looked at each other and frowned. But neither Zeke nor Hector could come up with a better idea, so off we went.

Don't get me wrong. Even though asking Melvin was the right thing to do, I wasn't as calm as I acted about confronting a bully.

But I'd never let Zeke know that.

We spotted Melvin by the playground equipment, menacing little kids with the Brush. My feet slowed. Hector and Zeke slowed even more, so I was in front.

But before we could reach Melvin, the custodian showed up. Mr. Wheener said something to the bully and put his hand out.

When Melvin didn't move quickly enough, the custodian spoke again. Sheepish, Melvin handed it over.

"That's our brush!" said Zeke.

"So why does Mr. Wheener want it?" I wondered.

"What does any normal person use a toilet brush for?" said Hector.

The custodian tucked the Brush under his arm and headed off toward his office.

"We've got to get it back," said Zeke.

I watched the janitor. "Later," I said. "After school, when nobody's here."

"You mean, the same 'after-school' when we're meeting with pirates and you're practicing with Mathletes?" said Hector.

"The same," I said.

"Dang," said Zeke. "Where's a time machine when you really need one?"

SORRY!

RIGHT, COME ON. *MARCH!*

CLIMB ABOARD.

YOU KNOW, I ALWAYS *WANTED* TO BE A *PIRATE.*

HERE'S YER CHANCE, LAD. PUT THIS ON!

COOL.

OVER YER EYES, *SQUID FACE.* NO ONE SEES OUR *HIDEOUT.*

A SHORT SAIL LATER...

I HOPE THEY'RE *FRIENDLY*.

FRIENDLY?

THEY'RE *PIRATES*.

ARRRR!

WHERE ARE WE?

UH, HI.

SORRY TO DROP IN LIKE THIS.

THEY WANTS TO SEE THE *CAP'N.*

THE CAP'N WILL *SEE 'EM,* ALL RIGHT—SEE 'EM WALKIN' THE *PLANK.*

GOOD IDEAR!

ARRRR!!!

ARE THE *CHOMPERS* READY?

YEP. HUNGRY, TOO!

WE WANTS THE *BOOTY!*

ARRR! WE WANTS THE *BOOTY!*

FRUITY BOOTY?

NARRR, BARNACLE BREATH. PIRATE BOOTY.

YOU WANT TO LOOT THE TOWN?

IT'S WHAT WE DO. WE ARE PIRATES, LUV.

NOW THEN, LASS, WHAT'S YER *PLAN?*

Wheener the Cleaner

Number concepts: Three kids have twenty-four hours to save the world. If it takes them eight hours for sleeping, six hours for school, three hours for eating and going to the you-know-where, one hour for homework, and eight minutes for feeding the cat, at what time will they have to leave home?

We popped out of the tunnel to Underwhere and ran for our bikes. There was no time to waste.

So of course a time waster showed up.

Dr. Prufrock stepped from his rattletrap car. "Children! By Bacchus's bib, where have you been?"

"Gotta run," I said, picking up my bike.

He stood in the driveway, blocking us. "But where's the, er"—he glanced over his shoulder—"*artifact*? Have you found it?"

"We had it," said Hector, stabbing a thumb at Zeke, "until *he* lost it."

"Hey," said Zeke.

I shot them a meaningful look. "We've got to get *going*."

"Where are you headed?" asked Dr. Prufrock.

"To find the—*ugh!*" Zeke stopped short. Probably because I elbowed him.

Just then, a long silver car pulled to a stop. Inside it sat the two government agents, Belly and Mole.

What *was* this, a time wasters' convention?

When Dr. Prufrock saw the men from H.U.S.H., he jumped and scrambled for his own car. They eyed him curiously.

"Let's *go!*" I hissed.

The spies were climbing out. "Where's our magical object?" said Agent Belly.

Pushing off, I steered my bike onto the sidewalk and pedaled down the street. I glanced back.

Zeke and Hector hadn't gotten away. Fine. They could sweet-talk the spies. I couldn't miss any more of Mathletes. I'd rather have twenty top-secret government agencies mad at me than face Mrs. Ricotta's disappointment.

As it turned out, I had to face it anyway. I made it to Mathletes practice only a half hour before the end. Mrs. R frowned, and half the team gave me dirty looks.

I flushed and sat down.

She *really* wasn't going to like it when I had to take a bathroom break in fifteen minutes to meet Zeke and Hector.

And she really, *really* wasn't going to like it when I told her I'd have to miss tomorrow's practice.

One thing at a time.

We did some speed drills adding and subtracting fractions. I aced them all. Then we moved on to geometry. When the time had come, I raised my hand.

"Mrs. Ricotta? May I go to the bathroom?"

She pursed her lips. "Now? Can't you wait?"

"It's really *urgent*," I said.

Mrs. R wasn't even impressed by my new vocabulary word. She sighed. "Very well. Hurry back."

Feeling like a traitor, I scooted out the door and down the hall. Zeke and Hector were waiting.

"Let's make this quick," I said. "Where's Mr. Wheener?"

"Haven't seen him," said Zeke.

We eased around the corner to the custodian's office. The door was closed. No light shone through the crack. Nobody walked the halls but us.

When we approached the office door, I had a *duh* moment.

"How do we get in without a key?" I asked.

Hector put a hand to the doorknob and turned it. "Like this," he said.

We poked our heads into the darkened room.

"I'd feel a heckuva lot safer knowing where Mr. Wheener is," said Zeke.

"Me too," I said. We looked down the hall again.

Hector pointed. "Isn't that his broom, by the boys' bathroom?"

We sneaked down the corridor to check it out. As we drew nearer, I noticed the bathroom door was propped open with a bucket of soapy water.

A rough voice sang something that sounded a little like *My Favorite Things*:

Blue silky boxers and fresh tighty-whities,
Big fancy bloomers and soft flannel nighties,
Scratchy old long johns that flap in the breeze,
These are a few of the greatest undie-e-es . . .

"Weird," whispered Zeke.

"But that's him, all right," I whispered. "Come on."

We rushed back to his office. Hector stood watch while Zeke and I turned on the light and looked around.

Push brooms and rakes leaned against the wall and sprawled on the floor. Dusty paint cans, old boots, and tubs of various cleansers sat here and there. Not like he ever *used* the cleansers. A half-cleaned brush drooled gold down the sink drain.

Cobwebs hung everywhere.

Yuck. I wouldn't hire Mr. Wheener to clean a hamster cage, much less a school.

"Over here," said Zeke. On a shelf of crusty sponges, the Brush lay with some other toilet brushes. He picked it up.

"Hurry!" said Hector. "I think he's coming."

Zeke stuffed the Brush under his T-shirt. I flipped off the light, and we eased the door shut.

Just in time. As we turned to walk away, something clattered behind us. Mr. Wheener's voice called, "You kids. Why you stay so late?"

I looked over my shoulder. "Um, we're Mathletes," I said.

He barked a short laugh. "Then you better get practicing. Otherwise, maybe everything don't add up." Mr. Wheener laughed again at his own joke.

I gave him a courtesy chuckle and hurried off with Hector and Zeke.

We parted just outside Mrs. Ricotta's classroom. "Now go straight home with that thing," I said.

"We will," said Zeke.

"And don't go rubbing it on anyone or showing it to anyone."

"What do you think we are?" he said. "Stupid?"

Hector held up a hand. "Don't answer that."

With no choice but to trust my brother, I shook my head and entered the classroom. Mrs. R said nothing, but she gave me a long look.

I sat down for the last few minutes of probability questions. But all I could think of was a probability question of my own.

How likely was it that Mrs. Ricotta would let me stay on the team when I told her I'd have to miss tomorrow's practice?

I knew the answer. And I didn't like it one bit.

Math Disaster

After thinking it over, I decided to give Mrs. R my bad news the next day. Maybe after a good night's sleep, she wouldn't mind it so much.

Maybe.

What with homework, dinner, and dishes, we didn't have time to try out the Brush that night. But I made sure it was safe. I hid it in our parents' room, just in case Zeke had another attack of the dumbs.

As we left for school the next morning, I told Caitlyn, "Don't forget the town meeting tonight."

"Yeah, about that dealie-o," she said, putting

cereal away. "I'm, like, not a thousand percent sure I'm gonna motorvate over there with you midgets."

"But you've *got* to!" said Zeke.

"I don't *have* to do diddley-whomp, you little dimweezil."

I shot Zeke a laser look. "What he means is, we *really* want you to get a good grade in that class, and we know that your report on the meeting will help."

"Uh, yeah," said Zeke. "It'd be a shame if you had to stop babysitting us because of bad grades. You're our favorite cousin."

Caitlyn's eyebrows lifted. But all she said was "If you zimwats want a ride, be on time or be, like, dead." She gave us a wave. "Toodles!"

We headed out the door and down the driveway. "'Favorite cousin'?" I said. "Think you were laying it on a little thick?"

122

"It's not too thick if she bought it. And she did."

I rolled my eyes. "Lucky thing you use your powers for good instead of evil."

At recess, I kept an eye on Mr. Wheener. Did he suspect we'd stolen back the Brush? It was hard to tell. He didn't act weird—well, no weirder than usual.

But bigger things occupied my mind. All through our lessons, I dreaded talking to Mrs. Ricotta about missing Mathletes.

I didn't get it. Helping the Undies was right; being in Mathletes was right. Why did I have to choose between the two rights, and why did it feel so wrong?

My stomach hurt. I barely ate any lunch.

Finally, the last bell rang, and everyone started packing up to go home.

"I'll see you Mathletes in ten minutes," said Mrs. Ricotta.

Zeke gave me a look and went outside. I wiped my hands on my jeans.

"Um, Mrs. Ricotta?" I said.

"Yes?" She looked up from the papers on her desk.

"I know I said yesterday would be the only time I'd miss practice, but . . ."

Her face fell. "Oh, no. You're not planning to skip *another* one?"

I nodded.

"Stephanie, you disappoint me. I thought you were committed to the team."

"I am," I said. "But . . . I've got other commitments. *Family* commitments."

She folded her hands. "Then I'm afraid you leave me no choice. Our first match is tomorrow. You can't miss today's practice and still be on the team."

"But—," I began, and stopped myself. "Whatever you think is fair."

Mrs. Ricotta shook her head.

I bit my lip, and then turned and left the classroom.

Zeke was waiting outside. "Way to go, Steph!" he said, patting my shoulder. "I knew you'd do what's right."

"Can you just not talk to me right now?" I said.

Heather gave me an accusing stare as I passed. I deserved it.

Zeke and I found Hector and hurried home. According to my calculations, we had just enough time to outwit the sea serpents, help the Undies take Port Heinie, make it back for the town meeting, and stop the UnderLord.

If all went well.

But the way my day was going, happy endings were the last thing I could count on.

'OWDY-DO, LOST PRINCE AND PRINCESS! AND UH...

LOST WHATCHA-MACALLIT.

WHAT? I'M *TIRED* OF TRYING TO FIGURE IT OUT.

RIGHT THEN, CAPTAIN. DO WE 'AVE A *DEAL?*

LET'S *SHAKE* ON IT!

ALL FOR ONE...

...AND ONE FOR...

ARRRRRRR!!

ARE THE *MIRRORS* AND *BOATS* READY?

AYE, PRINCESS.

THEN LET'S *SHOVE* OFF!

REMEMBER, DON'T START TILL THREE FORTY-FIVE!

COME ON, GUYS. LET'S START IT UP.

I THINK YE MEANS, 'HOIST THE MAINSAIL!'

SERPENT DEAD AHEAD!

WOOSH!!

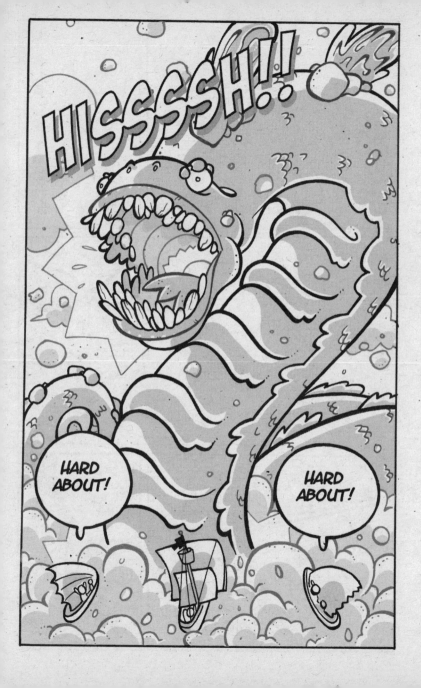

IF NOT, OUR NEXT *SCIENCE REPORT* IS ON WHAT'S INSIDE A *SEA SERPENT.*

HRRARRRSH!

CAN YOU SEE THE *BIG MIRROR* YET?

THERE IT IS!

RAISE THE *MIRROR!* SOUND THE CALL!

BLA-BLAAAHT!

PIRATES?! UH-OH!

NO WORRIES, MATE.

WHAT DO YOU *MEAN?* THEY'RE PIRATES!

BUT THEY CAN'T GET *UP HERE* WITHOUT LADDERS.

YOU WERE SAYING?

UH-OH.

ARRR!

FLUSH THE UNDERLORD!

AAAAHH!

CRACK!

BOOM!

TING!

A SHORT FIGHT LATER...

AND NOW?

BE MY GUEST!

CHAPTER

13

Bobby Bob's Big Surprise

We popped out of the portal and dashed for home. A kid on a bike saw us leave the construction site. But we couldn't worry about our secret getting out.

Caitlyn was waiting when we got home.

And Caitlyn didn't *like* to wait.

"I thought you little smigmotes *wanted* to go to this meeting!" she yelled as we ran up.

"We do," I said.

"*Well, it doesn't look like it!*" Caitlyn bellowed. "In the car! In, in, *in!*"

I held up one finger. "Bathroom?"

"At light speed!"

I had a funny feeling about the town meeting, so I dashed in, grabbed the Brush, and shoved it into my backpack. I may not be a Boy Scout, but it's only smart to be prepared.

All the way to City Hall, Caitlyn groused and groaned. She came up with some new insults to call us. Since I'm a princess, I won't repeat them.

A big mob crowded around the building. Caitlyn elbowed her way through to the front row. We followed.

At the top of the steps stood Mayor Rumley, a round man who looked like a beardless Santa Claus. Something big and lumpy lay covered up on a tabletop beside him.

"And here's the model for the new City Hall Mr. Moxenboxer is buying us," he said. The mayor pulled a sheet off the miniature building.

"Oooh!" went the people. Across the group, I

saw Dr. Prufrock. Even *he* looked impressed.

The model had more towers than the Taj Mahal, oodles of pillars, fountains, and a gold-colored roof. This was no city hall; *this* was a palace.

Zeke nudged me. "I wish the Undies would build *us* one of those."

"Here is the spa and Jacuzzi, and here's the garage for our new fleet of Mercedes," said Mayor Rumley, pointing at the model.

"Ahhh!" went the audience. Caitlyn scribbled on her notepad.

"And now, I'd like to introduce the man who's making this all possible: Mr. Bobby Bob Moxenboxer himself!"

Dressed all in green, Bobby Bob bounced up from his seat and approached the podium. He was so short, he disappeared behind it. Mr. Rumley coughed in embarrassment, and then scooted up a chair for him.

Bobby Bob stood on it and grinned at the crowd. He tipped his ten-gallon hat. "Howdy, friends!" he said.

"Howdy, Bobby Bob," the people replied.

"Howdy, cheapskate fake coin guy who's really the UnderLord," muttered Hector.

Just then I noticed the two government spies, Agent Belly and Agent Mole, standing off to the side.

"What, H.U.S.H.?" I said.

"Hush *yourself*," said Caitlyn. "I can't hear the dude."

I tuned back into what Bobby Bob was saying.

". . . Made a fortune in the plumbing biz," he drawled. "Bobby Bob's filthy rich, and he *lurrrves* this li'l ol' town so much, he wants to *buy* it from y'all."

Puzzled faces greeted his announcement.

"Oh, y'all can still live here—but Bobby Bob

will be your friendly landlord."

Dr. Prufrock spoke up. "So you want to *buy* our whole town?"

"Bull's-eye!" cried Bobby Bob. "And the City Council here has already given me the okeydokey."

I noticed the City Council members in their front-row seats. Their clothes looked brand-new and expensive. Jewelry glittered from their necks and hands.

Honestly. Some people like money *way* too much.

"How much are you offering?" asked an old lady from the crowd.

"Enough to make each and every one of you a *millionaire*!" said Bobby Bob.

The group erupted in cheers and argument. Everyone talked at once.

I huddled with Zeke and Hector. "The UnderLord wants to buy our town!"

"And it's not even for sale," said Hector.

Zeke scratched his head. "But why buy the town?"

"Well," I said. "If he owns everything, he could search anyone's house for the Throne or the Brush. He could search *our* house!"

"We've got to stop him," said Zeke. "But how?"

Suddenly, the mob roared. I looked up. Bobby Bob was tossing handfuls of gold into the audience.

"Fake coins *again*?" said Hector.

"That's it!" I said. "Let's show everyone that they're fake."

Zeke crinkled his forehead. "But don't we need . . ."

I reached into my book bag. "This?" I pulled out the Brush.

"Grab some of that gold," said Hector.

Luckily, Caitlyn had caught several coins.

"Omigod, I'm gonna be, like, totally mondo-*rich*!" she squealed. "Tiffany will scream her lungs out!"

"Can I see one of those?" I asked.

Her eyes narrowed. "What for?"

"It's very important," said Zeke.

"Okay," said Caitlyn, "but give it right back."

Zeke held the coin in his palm and I started rubbing the Brush over it.

"You might not want it back," said Zeke.

"Because as you can see," I said, "it's a *fake*!"

Caitlyn looked closely, then snorted. "Yeah, *right*, Steffo. You're gonna have to be trickier than that to separate *this* girl from her gold."

I gaped. The gold coin was still golden. But . . .

"That can't be," said Hector. "Mine was a fake."

Caitlyn grinned. "Well, *mine* isn't." She snatched her coin back.

Zeke stared at the Brush. I followed his glance, noticing the golden bristles, the painted handle with the frowny face . . .

Frowny face?

"I think I see the *real* fake," he said.

I gasped. "This brush isn't the Brush!"

"Sure," said Caitlyn, "it's a coffee pot. Now shut your faceplates, zimwats. I've gotta get this down on paper." She resumed her scribbling.

Hector frowned. "So if *this* brush isn't the real Brush, then that means . . ."

"We stole back a phony!" said Zeke.

"Mr. Wheener tricked us!" I said.

CHAPTER 14

Truth or Daring

"That little rodent!" said Zeke.

"*Big* rodent, actually," said Hector. "And who knows what he did with the *real* Brush?"

On the steps of the hall, Bobby Bob Moxenboxer was calling for order. "Mah friends! Now that y'all have seen the color of Bobby Bob's coin, let's vote."

My mind raced. We had to stall him until we could figure out how to unmask the UnderLord's plot.

I shouted out, "What if we have some questions?"

Bobby Bob scanned the crowd but didn't spot us. "Questions?" he asked. "Who in tarnation could have any questions about Bobby Bob's fine offer?"

A tall man raised his hand. "Actually, I've got one," he said. "Our million bucks—will it be cash or check?"

People laughed. While Bobby Bob answered, I grabbed Zeke and Hector.

"You guys create a diversion," I said.

"What are *you* going to do?" asked Zeke.

I raised the brush. "Get Bobby Bob to confess."

"But *that* brush doesn't make people tell the truth," said Hector. "It's fake."

"Maybe so," I said. "But *he* doesn't know that."

I started edging through the audience, working my way to the sidelines. If I could creep up on Bobby Bob before he saw me . . .

"Help! Somebody help!" cried Hector behind me.

I glanced back. He was bending over Zeke, who had fallen.

People crowded around. "What is it, sweetie?"

155

asked a curly-haired woman.

"My friend—he's real sick!"

"What's he got?" asked someone else, as Zeke twitched on the ground.

I kept moving. By now I was near the stairs.

"Um, boogie fever!" said Hector. "Stay back—it's contagious!"

Zeke's twitching got frenzied. He choked out, "Gack! Ga-gack-gack!" Then he jumped to his feet and started shaking his rear.

"Boog-oog, boogie-oogie-oogie!" he cried. "The g-g-groove has got me!"

Bobby Bob stared at Zeke, mouth open. Then a light went on in his eyes.

"Calm that scudder down!" he said. "Ah know that boy, and he's a pure-ol' troublemaker."

Caitlyn snagged Zeke's arm. She felt his forehead. "You're not sick, runt, but you're gonna, like, *wish* you were."

Mayor Rumley leaned into the microphone. "Settle down, folks. Let's get back to business."

Too many bodies blocked me from my target. I needed more time.

Hector noticed my problem. "Hey, mister," he called to Bobby Bob. "Where are you from?"

"Underwh— uh, from under the great flag of Texas, son," said the short man.

"Then you should be able to name the Texas state capital," said Hector.

Bobby Bob scowled. "Why, uh . . ."

"Austin," said Hector. "Or the state flower?"

"The, um . . ."

"Bluebonnet," said Hector. "Or the state serpent?"

"That's enough of this—," Bobby Bob retorted.

"Bull snake," said Hector. "You know, for a Texan, you sure don't know much about Texas."

I was only five feet from Bobby Bob. Time to make my move.

I dashed forward and raised the brush.

"Look out!" someone cried.

"The Brush!" shouted Dr. Prufrock.

Bobby Bob turned in time to see it descend. "The *Brush*?!" he shrieked.

I rubbed it on his back—once, twice, three times.

"Tell the truth," I said. "You're not really Bobby Bob, are you?"

The little man's eyes popped out. His face went red. "N-n-n-no, I'm not!"

"And that gold isn't real, is it?"

The phony Texan stuttered, "It's n-n-not!"

At that, the crowd gasped.

"It's fa—" Bobby Bob stopped and squinted. "Hey, that's no truth-telling spell." He spun and snatched the fake brush. "This isn't the Brush!"

I stepped to the mike. "He's the UnderLord," I said. "And he's not going to make you millionaires. He's trying to buy our town with fake gold!"

The mob booed and surged forward.

"You tryin' to swindle us, shrimp?" asked the curly-haired woman.

"You mean my gold's, like, totally *bogus*?" wailed Caitlyn.

The fake Bobby Bob Moxenboxer snarled. "A pox on all you Uplanders! And *you*"—he pointed at me—"you'll see me again. This isn't over!"

With that, he shook his right fist and shot out his fingers. "*Menthazar!*"

Powf!

Sparks showered. Blue smoke rolled over the podium and the surprised crowd. Coughing, I searched for the UnderLord.

But he was gone.

The mayor blinked. "Does this mean we're not getting our new City Hall?"

CHAPTER

15

Down the Drain Again

The next day, I didn't know how to feel. I'd never been so confused by trying to do right.

We had frustrated the UnderLord's plan, which was good. But we had lost the Brush to Mr. Wheener, which was bad. I had stood up for the Undies with Zeke and Hector—good. But I got kicked off the Mathletes team before our first match—really-bad.

At least one thing brought a smile. After the town meeting, we had passed the phony brush to the two spies. Let them run their high-tech tests on *that*!

All through class that day, Melvin kept smirking at Zeke and me. And this boy had one ugly smirk. Maybe he'd taken the Brush from us, but at least we could be thankful that this monkey brain didn't know about Underwhere.

After school, I went to watch the Mathletes compete. Amir and the others looked so smart in their red team shirts. But someone was missing.

"Mrs. R," I said, going up to her. "Where's Heather?"

"She's sick," said Mrs. Ricotta. "We'll have to compete without her."

"Let Stephanie take her place," someone said.

I turned around, and there was Zeke.

"She's missed two practices," said Mrs. Ricotta. "It wouldn't be fair."

He shook his head. "You don't understand. Steph is a math *freak*. She only missed practice because of *me*, and she just finished an awesome math project for the Un—uh, unbelievably lucky friends of ours."

Mrs. R looked at Zeke with a funny expression, but she said, "Okay."

I didn't wait to hear it twice. After donning a spare T-shirt, I joined the team.

The match went back and forth. We hit our dingers and shouted out our answers. In the end, our team won by a single point.

Afterward, Zeke and I walked home together.

"So," I said, "what did you think?"

"Nerd city," he said, raising a shoulder.

I smiled. We turned off Sycamore onto our street.

"You know," said Zeke. "I never thought I'd say this, but . . ."

"What? 'My sister is the smartest and prettiest girl ever'?"

"No, Steph-apotamus," he said. "That it's

actually good to have a day off from saving the planet."

Hector and Fitz came running up the sidewalk to meet us.

"Ree-eeow, rauw," Fitz yowled.

"Come quick, you guys!" cried Hector. He looked worried.

I flashed a glance at Zeke. "What is it?"

"Melvin," said Hector.

Zeke slumped. "What's he done now, stolen the Throne?"

"Worse," said Hector. "I was out looking for Fitz, and I found him in that construction site."

"Yes . . . ?" I said.

Hector hustled us up the street. "And you'll never guess who I saw there."

"Melvin," said Zeke. "Duh."

"*Duh*, yourself," said Hector. "Melvin has gone into Underwhere."

I stopped cold. "Oh, no."

"Oh, yes."

Zeke smiled and shook his head. "So much for that day off."

Basic math: One bully, plus a magical land, minus common sense, equals . . . big trouble.

"Guess we've got another problem to solve," I said.

Skivvies, take to the skies! Watch out below!

Turn the page for a peek at the third Underwhere adventure!

TOTALLY HILARIOUS!!!

FLYBOY of UNDERWHERE

BRUCE HALE   Illustrated by: SHANE HILLMAN

FlyBoy of UNDERWHERE

Everybody wants to be the hero; nobody wants to be the sidekick. It's true. Ask any two kids playing Batman and Robin, or Sherlock Holmes and Dr. Watson. Nobody wants to be Robin.

And the doctor? Forget about it.

(It's not just the dorky costume, either. Heroes get to be cool. Sidekicks get to tell the hero how cool *he* is.)

That's my problem. I don't want to be the sidekick. But sometimes I feel like I'm not even the hero of my *own* life.

If you've heard about our adventures from my buddy Zeke and his twin sister, Stephanie, you'll know that he's the Lost Prince of Underwhere (the place, not the cottony-fresh stuff you're wearing under your clothes). And Stephanie? She's the Lost Princess.

What am *I*? The Lost Cheese Wrangler, the Lost Beebee Stacker, the Lost Whatchamadingy.

It's my own fault. I just can't make up my mind about some stuff. And a hero should be able to make up his mind, right?

It's like that guy, Hamlet, said. "To be or not to be . . . something."

Let me explain.

My story starts with me nosing through the construction site, searching for Fitz, my talking orange cat. (He meows, sure, but he also talks English. More on that later.) Then I spotted something that looked like trouble.

Someone, actually.

Melvin Prang, school bully, was slipping into the secret passage to Underwhere, carrying a mysterious bag. Since Steph, Zeke, and I have been fighting to free Underwhere from the dirty rotten UnderLord and his pet zombies, this worried me.

Underwhere didn't need another bully.